The Magic Powder

It was a sparkling spring morning in Toy Town…

"Ahh! What lovely weather!" sighed Mr Sparks.
"It makes you want to sing and dance, doesn't it,
Noddy?"

"It certainly does! I – oh, my goodness!"

All of a sudden, Noddy slammed on the
brakes and jerked the steering wheel.

SCREEEECH! Noddy's little car skidded wildly
before coming to a standstill sideways across
the road.

Mr Sparks grabbed hold of his hat. Noddy's
head shook so hard his bell tinkled madly.

"W-w-what happened?" gasped Mr Sparks, looking very startled.

"Sorry, Mr Sparks," said Noddy. "Something leaped out in front of the car. I only just missed it – Oh!"

"*Woof-woof-woof!*" Two paws and an eager nose appeared over the top of the car door.

"It's Bumpy Dog!" cried Mr Sparks. "And he's very happy to see you, Noddy!"

Bumpy barked and started licking Noddy's nose.

But Noddy wasn't very happy. "Bumpy! I nearly crashed into you! Get DOWN!"

"Don't be too hard on him," said Mr Sparks. "He's only a puppy. He doesn't understand about traffic rules."

Bumpy took a flying leap into the car.
But Noddy was still cross.
"You shouldn't run out in front of cars,
Bumpy!" he scolded.
Bumpy Dog hung his head.

They were soon zooming along again towards
Toy Town. Then, all of a sudden, Bumpy Dog
jumped up at Noddy again.

"Get down at once, Bumpy!" shouted Noddy.
"You should never, EVER mess about in a car!"

Bumpy whined. He hated it when Noddy
was cross.

Poor Noddy. Something even worse was brewing
in Dark Wood. The two bad goblins, Gobbo
and Sly, were up to their usual tricks.

"Just two more things to add!" chortled Gobbo:

The sparkling laces of a ballerina's shoe,
The tapping rhythm of a drumstick true.
Dancing Potion, Dancing Potion,
Now you turn BLUE!

There was a FLASH! and the magic potion turned into sparkling blue powder.

Gobbo scooped up a handful. "Soon all of Toy Town will be dancing to our tune," he gloated.

"But Gobbo," whined Sly, "dancing's fun."

"They won't think it's fun when we've finished with them!" grinned Gobbo.

Soon Noddy stopped his car near Town Square.

"Thanks for the ride, Noddy," said Mr Sparks.

Bumpy was so excited that he jumped up again – and knocked Noddy over.

"Get DOWN!" Noddy cried. "Will you stop jumping and bumping all over the place?"

Poor Bumpy whined sadly and slunk away with his tail between his legs.

Just then, Noddy heard someone ringing a bell.

It was Gobbo the goblin.

"Roll up! Roll up!" yelled Gobbo. "Prepare to be AMAZED!"

What was Gobbo up to?

A crowd soon gathered to watch and Noddy joined them.

"No energy? Sore, aching feet?" cried Gobbo. "Never fear! I have here… a magic cure!"

And he waved towards a bottle full of sparkling blue powder.

"My Magic Comfort Foot Powder will put a spring in your step! You'll feel as if you're walking on air. One sprinkle and you'll be dancing in the streets!" Gobbo cried.

The Toy Town crowd murmured with surprise. Could they really trust Gobbo?

Just then, a stranger limped forward.

"Oooo, my feet are so-o-o sore," moaned the stranger. "I'd do anything to get rid of the pain."

"You won't be sorry, sir!" smirked Gobbo, as he pretended to sprinkle the powder over the stranger's feet.

"Wow!" Everyone gasped as the stranger leaped into the air and danced wildly across the stage.

The amazing dance convinced everyone.

"How much is that magic powder?" called out Mr Plod, the policeman.

"It's free… for one day only!" grinned Gobbo.

"It sounds too good to be true," said Noddy. "But I'll try some."

Soon, everyone had a bottle of Gobbo's Magic
Comfort Foot Powder and they sprinkled the
sparkling blue powder over their feet.

"Ooo, it feels lovely!" sighed Dinah Doll.

"Like I'm floating on air!" laughed Noddy.

Mr Plod smiled at Gobbo, "You've done
something good for a change! Thank you!"

"Only too happy to help!" smirked Gobbo as the crowd walked away. The stranger stayed behind.

"Can I take off my disguise now, Gobbo?" he asked. It was Sly!

Gobbo laughed. "Of course you can, Sly! Heh! Heh! They fell for our trick! All those silly people tried our magic foot powder. Now we just need a little tune!"

Sly turned the handle of their music box
and a lively tune filled the air. All at once, the
goblins' Magic Comfort Foot Powder began
to work its magic.

Feet began tapping and heads began
nodding as everyone broke into a wild, crazy
dance, twirling and whirling and spinning all
around the town.

The two naughty goblins roared with laughter.

"It's the funniest thing I've ever seen," gasped Sly.

"Now's our chance," said Gobbo. "They can't stop us stealing – they're too busy dancing!"

At Dinah Doll's stall, poor Dinah could only dance and scold as Gobbo filled his sack.

"Don't worry, Dinah, I'll arrest them!" cried Mr Plod, dancing towards the two goblins.

"Oh, no you won't!" Gobbo sniggered, as the music played even faster. Mr Plod could do nothing but dance, dance, dance!

"HELP!" he wailed, whirling down the street.

The goblins' music had set Noddy's feet dancing and his head nodding too.

"What a nice car!" said Gobbo as he climbed into Noddy's car.

"You leave my car alone!" cried Noddy angrily.

"What's that, Noddy?" sniggered Gobbo. "Can't stop dancing? Never mind. We'll have your car."

The gleeful goblins loaded Noddy's car with everything they had stolen.

"There isn't one person in Toy Town who can stop us!" chortled Gobbo.

But he was wrong.

At that moment, Bumpy Dog wandered sadly into the square. But when he saw Noddy, he bounded happily up to him – and knocked him right over!

"Bumpy! Why aren't you dancing?" cried Noddy, his feet still dancing in the air.

Bumpy barked.

"Of course!" Noddy laughed. "You don't have any magic powder on your paws so you aren't under the spell!"

He hugged Bumpy. "Now, go and stop those goblins!"

Bumpy leaped up at the two troublemakers and knocked the magic powder out of Gobbo's hands.

PUFF! A cloud of sparkling blue powder billowed out around them.

"Why, you pesky pooch, I'll – uh-oh!" Gobbo cried as his feet began to jiggle and wriggle.

Soon the two goblins were dancing furiously.

"Quick! Stop the music, Sly!" Gobbo shouted.

Sly stopped the music box and the goblins stopped dancing. But so did everyone else.

"Stop, in the name of Plod!" shouted the policeman as he ran towards them.

"Oops!" cried Gobbo. "You'd better start playing again, Sly!"

CRASH! Bumpy Dog knocked the music box out of Sly's hand and it smashed to pieces.

"Let's get out of here!" cried Gobbo. But it was too late!

Mr Plod grabbed both goblins. "Going somewhere?" he asked sternly.

"Heh, heh. To jail?" Sly said helpfully.

"You guessed it!" said Mr Plod.

"Well done, Bumpy, you're a hero!" said Dinah.
"You deserve that bone for saving us from those
naughty goblins."

"You're a great dog, Bumpy," cried Mr Sparks.

Then Bumpy bounded up to Noddy, wagging
his tail like mad.

"I'm sorry I was mean to you, Bumpy," said
Noddy. "Without all your jumping and bumping,
we'd still be dancing to the goblins' tune!
Are we still friends?"

Bumpy barked, leaped up at Noddy and…
knocked him off his feet.

"Oh, Bumpy!" laughed Noddy.

First published in Great Britain by HarperCollins Publishers Ltd in 2002

3 5 7 9 10 8 6 4 2

ISBN: 0 00 715101 2

Printed and Bound by Printing Express Ltd., Hong Kong

make way for

N⊙DDY

™

Collect them all!

Hold on to your Hat, Noddy
ISBN 0 00 712243 8

The Magic Powder
ISBN 0 00 715101 2

Noddy's Perfect Gift
ISBN 0 00 712365 5

Noddy and the New Taxi
ISBN 0 00 712239 X

Bounce Alert in Toy Town
ISBN 0 00 715103 9

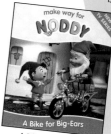

A Bike for Big-Ears
ISBN 0 00 715105 5

And send off for your free Noddy poster (rrp £3.99).
Simply collect 4 tokens and complete the coupon below.

TOKEN

Name: _____

Address: _____

_____

_____

e-mail: _____

❏ Tick here if you do not wish to receive further information about children's books.

Send coupon to: **Noddy Marketing, HarperCollins, 77-85 Fulham Palace Road, Hammersmith, W6 8JB.**

Terms and conditions: proof of sending cannot be considered proof of receipt. Not redeemable for cash. 28 days delivery. Offer open to UK residents only.

WATCH OUT FOR 'MAKE WAY FOR NODDY' ON VIDEO, AUTUMN 2002

UNIVERSAL